Irene Smalls

Don't Say Ain't

Illustrated by Colin Bootman

TALEWINDS
A Charlesbridge Imprint

"I wants my children to be educated because I can believe what they tells me. If I go to another person with a letter in my hand, he can tell me what he pleases in that letter and I don't know any better. But if I have got children who read and write, they will tell me the contents of that letter and I will know it's all right."

— A Louisiana freedman, from *The Trouble They Seen: Black People Tell the Story of Reconstruction*

For my Godmother, Louise Godfrey McNeil, who taught me "I Love You, Black Child."

— I. S.

To my daughter Rashida, her friends Kimberly and Vinell, and Sharon. A special thanks to B. Henoni for inspiring me in a way that no one else could.

— C. B.

Text copyright © 2003 by Irene Smalls
Illustrations copyright © 2003 by Colin Bootman
All rights reserved, including the right of reproduction in whole or in part in any form.
Charlesbridge, Talewinds, and colophon are registered trademarks of Charlesbridge Publishing, Inc.

A *TALEWINDS* Book
Published by Charlesbridge
85 Main Street
Watertown, MA 02472
(617) 926-0329
www.charlesbridge.com

Library of Congress Cataloging-in-Publication Data
Smalls-Hector, Irene.
    Don't say ain't/by Irene Smalls; illustrated by Colin Bootman.
        p. cm.
"Talewinds book."
Summary: In 1957, a young girl is torn between life in the neighborhood
she grew up in and fitting in at the school she now attends.
    ISBN 1-57091-381-1 (reinforced for library use)
[1. Schools—Fiction.] I. Bootman, Colin, ill. II. Title.
    PZ7.S63915 Do 2002
    [Fic]—dc21   2001004400

Printed in Korea
(hc) 10 9 8 7 6 5 4 3 2 1

Illustrations in this book done in oil on Bainbridge hot press board
Display type and text type set in Cochin and Sabon
Color separations by ArtScans Studio Inc., Manhattan Beach, California
Printed and bound by Pacifica Communications, Korea
Production supervision by Brian G. Walker
Designed by Susan M. Sherman

"Don't say ain't or your Momma will faint,
And your father will fall in a bucket of paint;
Your sister will cry till the fourth of July,
And your dog will call the FBI."

Dana's braids—one in front, two in back—beat in plait-
a-plait time. Dana flipped in the ropes while jumping.
Ellamae whistled with the great gap between her two
front teeth. Cindybelle hooted and stomped her feet.
Dana took a bow.

"Don't say ain't, children. People judge you on how you speaks!" scolded Dana's godmother, as she rushed past the girls.

She planted herself on the street corner and waved a letter at folks coming home.

"I'se got big news," Godmother shouted. "My baby's passed a test. Goin' to an advanced school! She's goin' to grow up to be a doctor!"

Cindybelle and Ellamae fell out laughing. Dana thought she was going to die of embarrassment. She dropped her end of the rope and made a dash for her tenement building. Dana skedaddled up the three flights to her apartment.

Dana made tea. Every evening Dana had tea and bread and talk with her godmother.

Godmother bustled in. "As I was sayin', speaking proper shows you gots a good education. Things ain't like dey was when I was a chile. This is 1957. Now you got a chance to go to a good school, get a good education, and get a good job."

Dana groaned. "But I don't want to go to any school away from my friends. Cindybelle, Ellamae, and I have been friends since kindergarten."

Godmother sighed. "Chile, you got the highest grade on the city test. You gone too far to fall back."

To change the subject, Dana got a book. She gently held Godmother's hand, showing Godmother the words as she read them.

On the first day of school, when Dana awoke, her glass of milk with a pinch of sugar in it was on the table with five different breakfasts. Dana ate well. She knew Godmother would just keep cooking things until Dana ate a full plate of something.

Dana carefully touched the hem of her best outfit, her yellow party dress. Godmother, up since dawn, had starched and pressed it for Dana to wear. Godmother rubbed petroleum jelly on Dana's scuffed dress shoes. "They're not perfect, chile, but they're better than they was," Godmother said, sniffling. Dana gave Godmother a peck on the cheek and quickly dressed, escaping.

Mornings before school the girls always met on the corner. Ellamae let out a high, soft whistle—*skee whee*—when she saw Dana, who giggled and said, "Time for reading, time for books . . ."

"Time for teachers' dirty looks," Ellamae sang back, laughing.

Cindybelle frowned, muttering to Ellamae, "She thinks she's better'n us cause she's goin' to that advanced school now." Ellamae stopped laughing and stared at Dana.

Dana didn't know what to say. She could only stare back as Cindybelle pulled Ellamae away toward Dana's old school.

Dana stumbled in the other direction to the advanced school.

At the advanced school, Dana's teacher, Mrs. Middleton, wore a suit, high-heeled shoes, and white gloves. All the girls wore pleated skirts and sweater sets. Everyone stared at Dana in her flouncy lace-and-satin party dress.

Mrs. Middleton moved her mouth when she talked as though she were chewing gum. The kids spoke the same way. Dana missed the running jive and banter, the way she and her friends talked. Dana felt as though her tongue were tied up with rope.

At recess Dana put on a smile and walked over to a group of girls. She pulled out her jump rope, saying, "I ain't the bestest, but I'll teach y'all to play double Dutch."

Mrs. Middleton, walking by, whispered, "Please, darling, do not use 'ain't' in school."

The girls sniggled, trailing behind Stephanie, who was talking about her tennis lessons.

Dana stood alone. She hid her rope behind her back.

Later, in class, no one could answer the last math problem. Dana sat on her hands, she knitted her fingers together, she bit her tongue, and she pursed her lips, but she couldn't keep quiet. Dana shakily raised one of her hands while she pinched pleats in her dress with the other. "The answer is two hundred and eighty-seven," Dana squeaked, articulating every word.

"Correct and well stated!" Mrs. Middleton said.
Stephanie yelped, "Huh?" Dana made a face at
Stephanie. Then Dana buried her head in her math book,
twisting her braid into a tight, tight knot.

The advanced school was shiny and new, with a language lab, a gym, and a big library. Dana laughed when her French teacher said, "Dana, you have a wonderful French accent!" In music class Dana patted her new flute proudly and tooted the loudest.

But in the days that followed, Cindybelle was never at the corner anymore. Ellamae came twice. Then she, too, stopped coming. Dana waited alone each day.

One morning, her teacher said, "I will be visiting each student at home. Dana, I will visit you first."

Dana dropped her book, flabbergasted. She didn't hear anything else for the rest of the day.

After school Dana hurried home. She raced up the stairs, exploding, "I hate the kids at that advanced school! And . . . and . . . the teacher's coming here Saturday." Dana put her head in Godmother's lap and cried.

Godmother patted Dana on the back, murmuring, "Chile, you gone too far to fall back."

On Saturday morning, when Mrs. Middleton came, Dana sat in the corner farthest from her teacher, her best Sunday school smile plastered on her face. To Dana's surprise, Godmother knew Mrs. Middleton's mother back in Charleston, South Carolina. It seemed like the "Honeychiles this" and "Honeychiles that" would never stop. The teacher took off her suit jacket and white gloves, laughing. "Honeychile, I ain't gonna eat more than one piece of your famous peach cobbler."

Godmother beamed. Dana squealed and jumped up when she heard her teacher say "ain't."

Godmother scowled. Dana gulped and said, "May I go outside?" She grabbed her rope and ran.

Cindybelle and Ellamae were dancing in front of the record shop. Dana hesitated and then slowly walked over. Cindybelle turned away; Ellamae gave a half smile.

"Hi," Dana said. "I wanted to invite yous to my really big party. Wanna come?"

Both girls nodded. "When is it?" Ellamae asked eagerly.

"Well . . . well . . . um . . . it's not till almost Christmastime, but I wanted to make sure that you two knew about it first," Dana answered.

"Oh," said Cindybelle, "that's a long way away," and went to sit on the fire hydrant.

Dana stammered, "M—my teacher's at the house."

"Oh? What did you do?" Ellamae asked, interested.

"Nothing," Dana answered.

Cindybelle sneered, "Miss Smarty Pants. Must be teacher's pet."

Dana, ignoring her, started talking faster. "You know what? My teacher talks strange at school, but then she talks like real people here! Ain't that funny?"

Ellamae said softly, "Go back to that school. We're not good enough for you."

Tears rolled down Dana's face. She clenched her rope. She wanted to run home. But Godmother and Mrs. Middleton were on the stoop. The teacher held out a white gloved hand and said, "Good-bye, dear."

"What!" Dana exclaimed. Her hands moved up and down her rope furiously. She thought about Mrs. Middleton saying "ain't" and then changing again. She thought about her godmother, her school, her friends. . . . It was all so confusing.

But Dana knew one thing for sure.

Dana slowly turned around and faced Ellamae. "I don't want to be all alone," Dana whispered. "I want us to be friends again."

Ellamae started to cry. "Why would you want us for friends?" she asked. "We're just . . . just . . ."

"Just the best and craziest friends ever," Dana answered.

Cindybelle walked up to Dana. "You don't think you're better'n us?"

Dana said, "Course not," and wiped her eyes. "Cindybelle is the best at double Dutch, Ellamae has the best whistle, and I'm good at math and stuff. So what?"

"Yeah, so what!" said Ellamae and began to sing, grabbing Dana and Cindybelle. "Boom boom. Ain't it great to be crazy. Boom boom. Ain't it great to be just like us!"

"Ooh, don't say ain't," Cindybelle said. The girls howled as they danced the Bop, the Slop, and the Mashed Potato.

Dana pulled out her rope, and Ellamae grabbed one end as Cindybelle grabbed the other. The girls played double Dutch.

Watching the ropes, Dana was lost in thought. Suddenly Dana yelled, "I gets it!"

"Gets what? That new school has you talking strange," Cindybelle teased.

Dana made a face at Cindybelle. "I gets it," she repeated.

Her turn jumping in the ropes, Dana sang a new song:

"If you want to say 'ain't,'
So people won't faint,
And laugh and think you're quaint,
Just say it at home.
And when you roam,
Speaking proper sets de tone,
So folks won't moan,
And dat's that."

"Girly girl, that don't even rhyme," Ellamae bantered.

Dana retorted, "It don't hafta rhyme. I've figured out when to say 'ain't' and whens to be proper. I've gone too far to fall back."